American edition published in 2014 by Andersen Press USA, an imprint of Andersen Press Ltd.
www.andersenpressusa.com

This paperback edition first published in 2009 by Andersen Press Ltd.
First published in Great Britain in 2006 by Andersen Press Ltd., 20 Vauxhall Bridge Road, London SW1V 2SA.
Published in Australia by Random House Australia Pty., Level 3, 100 Pacific Highway, North Sydney, NSW 2060.
Copyright © Tony Ross, 2006.
Distributed in the United States and Canada by Lerner Publishing Group, Inc.
241 First Avenue North Minneapolis, MN 55401 U.S.A.
For reading levels and more information, look up this title at www.lernerbooks.com.
Color separated in Switzerland by Photolitho AG, Zürich. Printed and bound in Malaysia by Tien Wah Press.
Library of Congress Cataloging-in-Publication Data Available.
ISBN: 978–1–4677–5095–0
ISBN: 978–1–4677–5096–7 (eBook)

This book has been printed on acid-free paper

MIX
Paper from
responsible sources
FSC   FSC® C012700
www.fsc.org

A Little Princess Story

I Want to Go Home!

Tony Ross

Andersen Press USA

One day, the Queen found a new castle.

"This one's too small, now that we have your brother!"

"And then, there's that lot," she said.

"And THAT LOT . . ."
"I don't want to live somewhere else,"
said the Little Princess.

"Oh, yes you do," said the Queen.
"You'll have much more room."

So, the Duke of Somewhereorother
bought the old castle . . .

. . . and the Little Princess moved into the new one.

"I WANT TO GO HOME!" said the Little Princess.

"You ARE home," said the Queen. "Look at your posh new room. It's big and full of your things."

"I WANT TO GO HOME!" said the Little Princess.

"But look at the new yard," said the Queen.
"Perhaps the Gardener will let you help him."

"I WANT TO GO HOME!" said the Little Princess.

"But look at the new kitchen," said the Queen.
"I want to go home NOW!" said the Little Princess.

"Very well," said the Queen. "You can go back
to the old castle, but only for a peep."

"The Duke of Somewhereorother lives
there now. Look, he's painted it!"

"The Dukelet lives in your old room!"

"Look at the lovely new kitchen!"
said the Duchess of Somewhereorother.

"And see how nice the yard is
without those horrible trees . . ."

"We could have tea and cake on the lawn . . .

. . . so long as you don't drop crumbs."

"After all, we don't want birds, do we? I have
to vacuum the grass every day as it is."

"I WANT TO GO HOME!" said the Little Princess.
"ME TOO!" said the Queen.

"There's no place like home!" said the Little Princess.

Other Little Princess Books

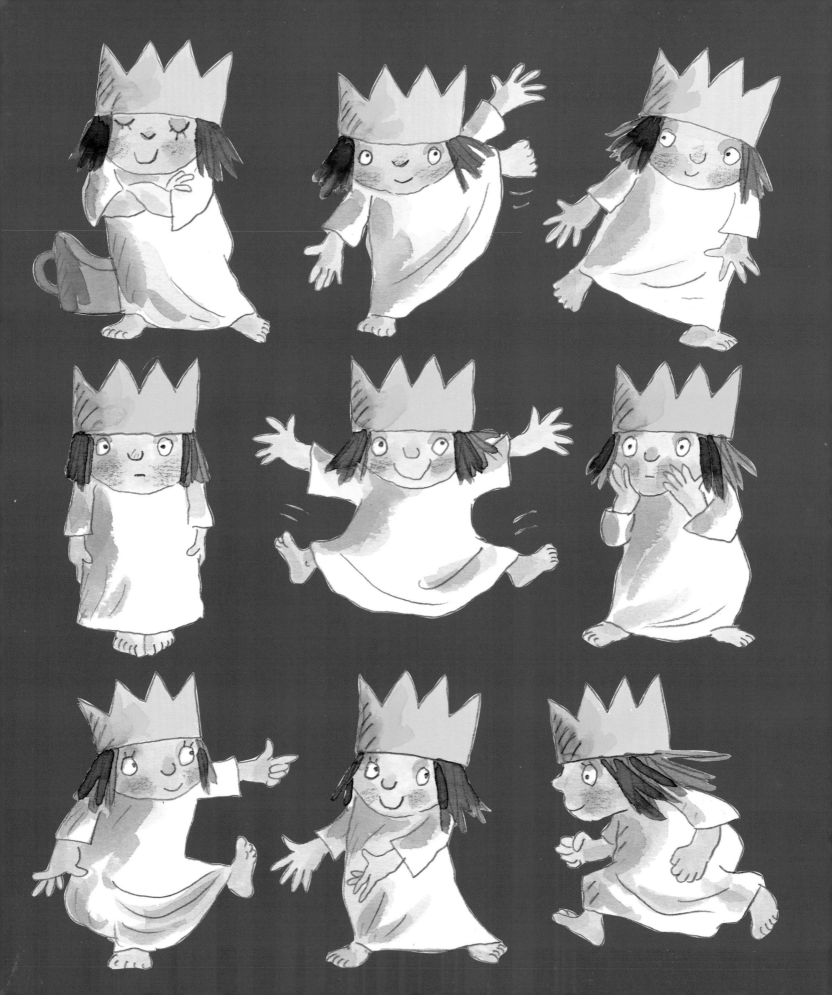